Design by Roger Handling

NIGHTWOOD EDITIONS
P.O. Box 219
Madeira Park, BC Canada V0N 2H0

Canadian Cataloguing in Publication Data

White, Howard, 1945–
Patrick and the backhoe

ISBN 0-88971-052-X

I. Griffiths, Bus, 1913–   II. Title.
PS8595.H58P3 1991   jC813'.54   C87-091389-1
PZ7.W495Pa 1991

Printed in Canada

◆ PATRICK ◆

AND THE BACKHOE

BY HOWARD WHITE ◆ ILLUSTRATED BY BUS GRIFFITHS

Patrick and Simon lived in a little town on the side of a high mountain. The town was called Cypress. It had a town hall, a church, a supermarket, a bank, a gas station, a library, a school, and a bookstore. The road to the town passed over a bridge, and under the bridge ran Cypress Creek.

Patrick and Simon were brothers but they were different as night and day.

Simon liked to read books and draw pictures.

Patrick liked to take things apart and climb up on things. The only book he liked was *Mike Milligan and His Steam Shovel*, which he always kept under his pillow. Mostly he liked to make things work. That was why he always asked his father to let him turn the light switch on. Switches made things go on and off.

Patrick always asked to turn the key. Keys made the door open and made the car go.

Patrick liked knobs and levers, too. Knobs made the radio work, and levers made the washing machine go.

Patrick liked to take all the keys and knobs and levers and keep them under his pillow. When Dad and Mom couldn't make something work because the key was missing, it usually turned out Patrick had it.

Patrick was always learning how to make things work, mostly things his mom and dad didn't want him to work. Once when he was quite small he learned how to make the door of the car work when Dad was driving, and he fell out on his noggin. He had to go see the doctor after that.

"Well, Patrick! You look like you were fighting with a bear!" the doctor said. "What did you turn on this time?"

Patrick didn't answer because he was too busy turning on the doctor's X-ray machine.

Patrick's mom and dad were always busy talking to people in the bookstore. Simon was always busy putting his hockey cards in a book.

Patrick couldn't think of anything to do. He had already secretly turned off the furnace and turned on the store's outside sign and locked the keys inside the car and changed the date on the credit card machine and rung up nine hundred and fifty-six trillion, seven hundred and eighty-eight billion, three hundred and thirty-nine million, two hundred and seventy-nine thousand, six hundred and fifty-seven dollars on the cash register while Mom was in back mopping up the water he'd overflowed by flushing a stuffed dog named Snuffy down the toilet.

Patrick was bored because he thought there was nothing to do in a bookstore. His dad was mad because he thought Patrick found too much to do in the bookstore, and they were all the wrong things.

"Why can't you be more like your brother?" his dad and mom said together. Simon was in the reference section where he'd spent hours quietly searching the animal books for pictures of tarsiers. Mom and Dad were always telling Patrick to be more like Simon, and whenever they did, it made Patrick want to stuff his brother's hockey cards down the furnace

4

grating. When Simon caught him he would shriek with horror and lunge at him like a wild animal, fists flying. Patrick would fight back as best he could and Dad would would run back and angrily pull them apart, saying the boys were scaring customers out of the store.

"I don't know what to do about those two," he would say to Mom, shaking his head.

It happened all the time.

Patrick heard something that made him run to the window with a big smile on his face. It was the noise of Grampa's backhoe coming down the street: putt-putt-putt. Patrick loved Grampa's old backhoe because it had more levers and knobs and buttons on it than anything in the world. He loved it even more because it dug up the buried pipes and wires that wriggled around in the ground underneath Cypress bringing the water and power that made everything in the town work.

Mom loved it when Grampa came on his backhoe because Patrick would stand outside on the sidewalk for hours contentedly watching Grampa dig up the pipes and wires and not getting into mischief. Grampa always waved when he saw Patrick and sometimes he let him ride up and down in the bucket, away up in the air, just like a ride at Playland. Grampa's old dog Jason would ride up with them, barking his fool head off.

Several months before, mean Mrs. McCracken saw Patrick having fun in Grampa's backhoe and put a stop to it. She said it was not right for children to play on a backhoe. She also said Jason was dirty and shouldn't be near children.

Grampa said to Patrick, "I think Mrs. McCracken is jealous because you had a ride and she didn't." He turned to Mrs. McCracken and said, "Mrs. McCracken, if you want a ride just jump in!" Jason licked Mrs. McCracken's hand. Mrs. McCracken shrieked and stomped away to the bookstore, dragging Patrick by the arm. Mom and Dad were very upset because they rented their store from Mrs. McCracken, and they were afraid she would throw them out.

"Never go near Grampa's backhoe again," Dad said with a worried look.

Patrick was sad, but what he really liked to do was watch Grampa work all the levers and knobs and wheels that made the backhoe's tires go round and its feet go up and down and its arm go in and out and its bucket go empty and full. When

Patrick went to sleep he dreamed about all those levers working all those things. There was nothing he wanted more than to someday get up on the seat of the backhoe and make everything work.

This day Grampa drove his old backhoe clankety-clank, putt-putt-putt straight down the street with Jason in the bucket barking his fool head off and stopped it across from the bookstore in front of Mrs. McCracken's house.

Patrick jumped up and down with excitement.

"Can I go out? Can I Mom? Can I?" he said.

"Alright," she said. "But don't go near the backhoe."

When Patrick ran across the road and took up his place on the sidewalk, Jason staggered over and licked him on the face. Jason's nose was awful and warty but his tongue was soft and warm. Grampa saw Patrick and gave him a big wave.

Just then Mrs. McCracken came running out waving her arms.

"What are you doing! You can't park that dreadful thing in front of my house!" she shrieked at Grampa.

"But I have to dig here to fix the sewer pipe," Grampa said.

"DIG! You'll do nothing of the sort!" Mrs. McCracken shrieked.

"But I have to clear the pipe. It's blocked between your house and the bookstore," Grampa said, pulling levers and taking a big bite out of the road.

Mrs. McCracken stomped off to get big fat Mr. Pie, the policeman. Grampa kept working levers and knobs and Pat-

rick kept watching until the sewer pipe was bare in the hole.
Then Grampa got down with his wrench to find out what was
blocking the pipe.

"AHA!" he said in a minute. "Here's what was blocking my
pipe." He held up a smelly lump of mud that looked like it was
once a stuffed toy.

"Snuffy!" Patrick cried, hugging the mucky toy puppy.

Just then Mrs. McCracken came back up the street with
fat Policeman Pie, who was as round as a pie.

"There!" she fumed, pointing at Grampa. "Just look at the
mess that horrible old man has made in front of my house!"

"Halt!" boomed Mr. Pie. Grampa climbed down from the backhoe looking worried.

"You come with me!" Mr. Pie roared, taking Grampa by the arm. "The mayor wants to talk to you!"

"But I left my backhoe's motor on," Grampa said. "At least let me turn the motor off."

"Don't let him!" shrieked Mrs. McCracken.

"My backhoe might be ruined if I leave the motor running," Grampa said.

"Good!" said Mrs. McCracken. "It's time we got one of the big new backhoes to fix our pipes. Your backhoe is too old and so are you!"

Policeman Pie dragged Grampa away as Mrs. McCracken followed behind him jabbering like a crow and Jason followed behind her barking his fool head off.

Patrick was left alone with the backhoe. It looked lonely putt-putting away by itself with Grampa nowhere in sight. Patrick felt very sad. He decided he had to do something for his old friend, even if it meant going somewhere he wasn't supposed to. Slowly he climbed up onto the seat of the backhoe. He looked at all the handles and levers and buttons and knobs and tried to remember which one he saw Grampa using to turn the motor off. The middle lever he knew was to lower the arm. Beside it was the one that turned the bucket. Beside that was the one that lowered the feet. As he looked at each lever a little thrill rose up inside him, and one little thrill piled up on another little thrill until his sadness went away.

He couldn't resist. He put his hand on the lever that made the arm swing sideways. The backhoe jumped and shook and the arm swung, but it swung the wrong way. Before Patrick could stop it, it was reaching right out over Mrs. McCracken's house. Patrick didn't like the looks of this. He pulled the lever he thought would move the backhoe arm back over the street. With an enormous crash the bucket plunged down through the roof of Mrs. McCracken's house, sending up a cloud of white dust. A stripey orange cat shot out through the hole as if from a gun.

Patrick smelled trouble now. He pulled the lever he

thought would take the bucket out of Mrs. McCracken's bedroom, but instead the backhoe pulled the front wall off the house, exposing all of Mrs. McCracken's private belongings to the street. Every table and cupboard and windowsill was covered with jars full of coins and dollar bills she had collected from the people of Cypress.

After that fateful day when Patrick wrecked Mrs. McCracken's house he never saw Grampa again. Mom said Grampa lost his job working on the town's pipes because of what Patrick did. Mrs. McCracken had tried to throw Mom and Dad out of the store, but agreed to let them stay if they paid three times as much rent and kept Patrick inside the store at all times. The shiny new backhoes came down the street now, but they didn't putt and clank like Grampa's did, and they didn't have all sorts of levers and knobs. They were noiseless like a new car, and the driver sat behind behind glass windows listening to stereo tapes and twiddling a silly-looking little lever between his fingers.

Patrick missed his old friend. He also missed going outside to play. He sat looking at his Mike Milligan book and gazing sadly down the street at the rain wondering where Grampa and Jason and the backhoe had gone.

It had been raining for weeks. Rain was all the grownups talked about. They were worried it would wash out the bridge, and maybe the town as well. Every day the rain poured down the mountain and into Cypress Creek. Every day the creek rose higher and surged more wildly under the bridge. Then a big boulder came loose and rolled down the hill, plugging the hole under the bridge. Now the raging waters of Cypress Creek backed up and began to wash away the land on which the town was built. Mom and Dad and Mrs. McCracken and Policeman Pie were now sure they would all be washed into the sea, but the flooding waters had cut off the bridge and nobody could escape.

"We must get a backhoe to dig out the boulder that is plugging the hole under the bridge," the mayor said. The people turned to the man who owned the new backhoe.

"Can you dig out the boulder?" they asked.

"Not on your life," said the man. "It is too dangerous and I might ruin my new backhoe."

"What will we do?" everyone said. The runaway creek had already washed away much of the land under the town. All the mothers and fathers looked very worried. All the children were crying. The houses would soon start to fall into the rushing waters and disappear out to sea.

Then Patrick heard a familiar sound. Putt-putt-putt, it went. He ran to the window. It was Grampa coming down the street in his old backhoe with his old dog Jason in the bucket, not barking his fool head off. The old backhoe stopped where the mayor and all the people had gathered looking at the boulder stuck under the bridge.

"My backhoe is old and I am old, but I would like to try to dig out that boulder and save the town," Grampa said. Mrs. McCracken looked at him angrily, but she didn't say any of the mean things she was thinking. Somebody had to dig out the boulder and save the town. The mayor shrugged and told Grampa he could try if he wanted.

Everyone in the town ran out to the edge of the cliff to watch. Mom and Dad and Simon and Patrick went too. They all saw Grampa drive out to the crumbling edge of the land and reach out the arm of the backhoe into the roaring water. But the old backhoe couldn't reach quite far enough to move the boulder.

"I will have to put a chain around it," Grampa said. Then he crawled along his old backhoe's outstretched arm over the roaring waters, a chain looped over his shoulder. Very carefully he stepped down onto the boulder. Very carefully he tied the chain around the boulder. Then just as he turned to climb back on the arm of the backhoe, the boulder shifted. The crowd gasped as they saw the old man stumble and the water fly up around him. They gasped again as the water cleared and they saw that he was still hanging on. But the boulder had rolled away from the arm of the backhoe and Grampa could not get back on it.

He was stuck on the rock.

"We are lost!" groaned the mayor.

"Our last hope is gone!" moaned Policeman Pie.

Jason whimpered, as a big tear rolled down his warty old nose.

"It serves you all right...!" spluttered Mrs. McCracken. She didn't know quite why it served them right, but she was very sure it did just the same.

All the people were so busy watching Grampa they did not see a little boy named Patrick run to the crumbling bank where the old backhoe teetered over the leaping waters. But everyone noticed when he climbed up on the seat and reached  for the levers that moved the arm. People began pointing and yelling.

"Get down from that backhoe this minute!" boomed Policeman Pie, standing safely back from the edge.

Patrick looked at the levers. He knew exactly which one made the arm go down—the same one he had pushed to make it go through Mrs. McCracken's roof. He pushed it again.

Clank!

The arm of the backhoe dropped to the rock where Grampa could reach it. He crawled toward it, hooked up the chain, and inched his way back up the arm to the seat where Patrick stood at the controls.

He let the boy sit on his lap as he pulled the lever that lifted the big boulder up and unplugged the hole under the bridge. With a roaring splash that shook the ground, the creek surged back into its proper channel under the bridge and the land under the town stopped washing away.

All the people sighed with relief. Then when Grampa and Patrick climbed down from the backhoe, all the people cheered.

"You have saved our town," said the mayor.

"It was young Patrick who really saved us," said Grampa.

"You both saved us," said the mayor. "And to show our appreciation we will give you anything you want. How about a nice long holiday to somewhere dry?"

"No thank you," said Grampa.

"How about if we give you a nice pension so you never have to dig again? We will mount your old backhoe in a place of honour on Main Street."

"No thank you," said Grampa.

"Well, what would you like, then?" said the mayor.

"I know I am old," said Grampa, "but there is nothing I would like more than to look after the pipes and cables that wriggle around under this town and make everything work."

"Is that all?" asked the mayor.

"Not quite," said Grampa, placing an arm around Patrick. "I want my little partner here to come with me whenever he feels like it."

"Why of course," said the mayor.

So Grampa got his job back and whenever it wasn't raining Patrick rode along with him and Jason helping to pull the levers and turn the knobs and switch the switches on the backhoe.

Even though one was very old and one was very young, they both liked to make things work.

HOWARD WHITE was born in Abbotsford, BC in 1945.
He started the regional journal *Raincoast Chronicles* in
1972, which led to the founding of Harbour Publishing.
He is the author of *A Hard Man to Beat* (with Bill
White), *The Men There Were Then* (poems) and *Writing
in the Rain*, which was awarded the 1991 Stephen
Leacock Medal for Humour. He lives in Pender
Harbour, BC with his wife and two sons.

G.J. (BUS) GRIFFITHS was born in Moose Jaw,
Saskatchewan in 1913 and his family moved to the BC
coast in 1922. He has been a logger since the early
1930s. He and his wife Margaret have two grown sons
and live in Fanny Bay, BC. He is author and illustrator
of the comic-book novel *Now You're Logging*.